John Alexander Martin

The Wyandotte convention; an address

John Alexander Martin

The Wyandotte convention; an address

1st Edition | ISBN: 978-3-75244-437-7

Place of Publication: Frankfurt am Main, Germany

Year of Publication: 2020

Outlook Verlag GmbH, Germany.

THE WYANDOTTE CONVENTION AN ADDRESS,

Delivered By

JOHN A. MARTIN,

THE WYANDOTTE CONVENTION.

MR. PRESIDENT:

It is often charged that participants in assemblages of this character are apt to exaggerate the importance of the occasion they commemorate, and after the manner of one of our poets, sing in chorus: "I celebrate myself." Perhaps I can speak of the Wyandotte Convention and its work without being accused of this self-gratulation; for I was more of an observer of its proceedings than a participant in them. I recorded what was done, but I had no part or lot in the doing. If its work had been crude or weak, I could not fairly have been held responsible for the failure. As it was strong, efficient and enduring, I can felicitate you, the survivors of those who wrought this great service for Kansas, without a suspicion of self-praise.

KANSAS CONSTITUTIONAL CONVENTIONS.

Four Conventions framed Constitutions for this State. The first assembled at Topeka, on the 23d of October, 1855, and adjourned on the 11th of November, after a session of twenty days. It was composed of forty-seven members, of whom thirty-one signed the Constitution. On the 15th of December this instrument was submitted to the people for ratification or rejection. Only 1,777 ballots were cast, all but 46 being favorable. One of its sections, a provision excluding negroes and mulattoes from the State, was submitted as an independent proposition, and adopted by an affirmative vote of 1,287, to 453 against it.

The second convention was that held at Lecompton, which met on the 7th of June, 1857, and after a session of four days, adjourned until the 19th of October, a final adjournment being reached on the 3d of November. It was composed of sixty-four members, forty-five of whom signed the organic law it framed, and its session continued twenty days. No direct vote on this Constitution was provided for. The Schedule ordered two forms of ballot, one, the "Constitution with Slavery," the other, "Constitution with no Slavery." It was the old turkey and buzzard choice. The Free State men refused to vote at the election, held on the 21st of December, and only 6,712 ballots were cast, 6,147 being for Slavery and 569 against Slavery. The Free State men had, however, elected a majority of the Territorial Legislature in October, and at a special session of that body, held in December, a law was passed providing for a direct vote on the Constitution. This election was held on the 14th of January, 1858, resulting: against the Constitution, 10,266; for, 164—the pro-Slavery men not voting. A third vote on the Lecompton instrument was taken August 2d, 1858, Congress having ordered its re-submission under the terms of the English bill. Again it was rejected, the ballots in its favor being only 1,788, and those against it, 11,300.

The Leavenworth Convention met at Minneola, March 23d, 1858, and at once adjourned to Leavenworth, where it re-assembled March 25th. It was composed of ninety-five members, was in session only eleven days, and the Constitution it framed was signed by eighty-three persons. This instrument was adopted at an election held May 11th, by a very small vote, the pro-Slavery men taking no part in the contest. It was never a popular organic law, and many Free State men who supported it did so under protest. An earnest effort was made, by the Republicans, to secure the admission of Kansas under the Topeka Constitution, and by the Democrats, with a few exceptions to bring the Territory in under the Lecompton Constitution. But no serious or determined contest was waged, in Congress, for admission under the Leavenworth Constitution, and in less than eight months the movement in its

3

behalf was formally abandoned.

THE WYANDOTTE CONVENTION.

Early in February, 1859, the Territorial Legislature passed an act submitting to the people the question of calling a Constitutional Convention. This vote was taken March 28th, and resulted: For, 5,306; against, 1,425. On the 10th of May, 1859, the Republican party of Kansas was organized, at Osawatomie, and at the election held on the 7th of June, for delegates to the Wyandotte Convention, the Republican and Democratic parties confronted each other in Kansas for the first time. The Democrats carried the counties of Leavenworth, Doniphan, Jefferson and Jackson, and elected one of the two delegates from Johnson. The Republicans were successful in all the other Counties voting. The total vote polled was 14,000. The Republican membership was thirty five; Democratic, seventeen.

The Convention then chosen assembled on the 5th day of July, 1859. In its composition it was an unusual, not to say remarkable, Kansas assemblage. Apparently the chiefs of the contending parties had grown weary of Constitution making, or regarded this fourth endeavor in that line as a predestined failure, for they were conspicuous by their absence. In the Topeka Convention nearly every prominent man of the Free State party had a seat. Gen. Lane was its President, and Charles Robinson, Martin F. Conway, Marcus J. Parrott, Wm. Y. Roberts, Geo. W. Smith, Philip C. Schuyler, C. K. Holliday, Mark W. Delahay, and many other recognized Free State leaders, were members. In the Leavenworth Convention there was a similar gathering of widely-known Free State men. Conway was its President, and Lane, Roberts, Thos. Ewing, jr., Henry J. Adams, H. P. Johnson, S. N. Wood, T. Dwight Thacher, P. B. Plumb, Joel K. Goodin, A. Larzalere, W. F. M. Arny, Chas. H. Branscomb, John Ritchey, and many other influential Free State chiefs or partizans, were among its members.

THE MEMBERSHIP.

In the Wyandotte Convention all the noted Free State leaders were conspicuously absent. Its roll-call was made up of names generally new in Kansas affairs, and largely unknown in either the Free State or pro-Slavery councils. Its President, James M. Winchell, his colleague, Wm. McCullough, and John Ritchey, of Shawnee, had been members of the Leavenworth Convention; Col. Caleb May, of Atchison, and W. R. Griffith, of Bourbon, had been members of both the Topeka and the Leavenworth Conventions; and Jas. M. Arthur, of Linn, had been a member of the Topeka Convention. But their prominence was largely local. On the Democratic side, too, appeared men before unnoted in the annals of the stirring and tremendous conflict that had for years made the young Territory the cynosure of a Continent's interest. None of the prominent pro-Slavery men who sat in the Lecompton Convention or the pro-Slavery Legislatures—Calhoun, Stringfellow, Henderson, Elmore, Wilson, Carr and others—appeared in this body.

Perhaps the absence of these party leaders was a fortunate thing for the Convention and the incipient State. For in discriminating intelligence, in considerate zeal for the welfare of the people, in catholic grasp of principles, and in capacity for defining theories clearly and compactly, the members of this body were not wanting. On the other hand, there were fewer jealousies and far less wrangling than would have been possible had the envious and aspiring party leaders been present. I think it is certain that the work was better done, done with more sobriety, sincerity, prudence and real ability, than would have resulted had the recognized chiefs of the rival parties been on the floor of the Convention. The pioneers—the John Baptists—of the Free State cause were all at Topeka, and the Constitution they framed is disfigured by some blotches and much useless verbiage. The leaders were all at Leavenworth, where they schemed for precedence, and spread traps to catch one another, and quarreled over non-essentials, and did everything but make a popular Constitution. Lecompton was the last expression of a beaten, desperate and wrong-headed, but intellectually vigorous faction, and was really, barring the mean method of its submission, and its attempt to perpetuate Slavery, an admirable organic law.

The younger men of the Territory constituted the Convention at Wyandotte. They came upon the field fresh, enthusiastic, and with a place in the world of thought and action to conquer. They recognized the fact that they must do extremely well to secure popular favor, and they set about their task with industry, intelligence and prudence. They were not martyrs or reformers, as many of those at Topeka were; nor jealous politicians or factionists, as most of those at Leavenworth were. They had no old battles to fight over again, no personal feuds to distract them, no recollection of former defeats or victories to reverse or maintain. They were their own prophets. They had had no experience in Constitution making, and hence did not look backward. They were not specialists. A few had hobbies, but the vast majority had no bees buzzing in their bonnets. A few were dogmatic, but the many were anxious to discuss, and willing to be convinced. A few were loquacious, but the majority were thinkers and workers. Some were accomplished scholars, but the majority were men of ordinary education, whose faculties had been sharpened and trained by the hard experience of an active and earnest life. Many were vigorous, direct, intelligent speakers; several were really eloquent; and a few may justly be ranked with the most versatile and brilliant men Kansas has ever numbered among her citizens.

Very few were old men. Only fifteen of the fifty-two members were over forty. Over one-third were under thirty, and nearly two-thirds under thirty-five. Very few, as I have said, had previously appeared as representatives of the people in any Territorial assemblage, and this was especially true of the men whose talents, industry and force soon approved them leaders. Samuel A. Kingman had been in the Territory only about eighteen months, and was unknown, outside of Brown county, until he appeared at Wyandotte. Solon O. Thacher was a young lawyer of Lawrence, never before prominent in public affairs. John J. Ingalls had served, the previous winter, as Engrossing Clerk of the Territorial Council. Samuel A. Stinson was a young attorney, recently from Maine. William C. McDowell had never been heard of outside of Leavenworth, Benjamin F. Simpson was a boyish-looking lawyer from Miami county, and John T. Burris had been practicing, for a year or two, before Justices' courts in Johnson county. John P. Slough had been a member of the Ohio Legislature, but was a new comer in Kansas; and E. G. Ross was the publisher of a weekly newspaper at Topeka.

One-half of the members had been in the Territory less than two years. Six came in 1854, four in 1855, and twelve in 1856, while Mr. Forman, of Doniphan, dated his residence from 1843; Mr. Palmer, of Pottawatomie, from 1854, and Mr. Houston, of Riley, from 1853. Forty-one were from Northern States, seven from the South, and four were of foreign birth, England, Scotland, Ireland, and Germany each contributing one. It appears singular that only one of the Western States, Indiana, was represented in the membership, that State furnishing six delegates. Twelve hailed from New England, Ohio contributed twelve, Pennsylvania six, and New York four. Only eighteen belonged to the legal profession—an unusually small number of lawyers in such a body. Sixteen were farmers, eight merchants, three physicians, three manufacturers, one a mechanic, one a printer, one a land agent, and one a surveyor. The oldest member was Robert Graham, of Atchison, who was 55;

7

the youngest, Benj. F. Simpson, of Lykins Co., (now Miami,) who was 23.

A WORKING BODY.

It was a working body, from the first hour of its session until the last. There is a tradition that the Continental Congress which promulgated the Declaration of Independence was materially hastened in its deliberations over that immortal document by swarms of flies that invaded the hall where it sat, and made the life of its members a burden. Perhaps the intense heat of the rough-plastered room where the Convention met, or the knowledge that Territorial scrip would be received by importunate landlords only at a usurious discount, had something to do with urging dispatch in business. But certainly the Convention went to work with an energy and industry I have never seen paralleled in a Kansas deliberative body since that time. It perfected its organization, adopted rules for its government, discussed the best mode of procedure in framing a Constitution, and appointed a Committee to report upon that subject, during the first day's session; all the standing Committees were announced on the third day; and by the close of the fifth day it had disposed of two very troublesome contested election cases, decided that the Ohio Constitution should be the model for that of Kansas, perfected arrangements for reporting and printing its debates, and instructed its Committees upon a number of disputed questions. The vote on selecting a model for the Constitution was, on the second ballot: for the Ohio Constitution, 25 votes; Indiana, 23; and Kentucky, 1. So our Kansas Constitution was modeled after that of Ohio—something, I think, as the farmer's new house was designed after his old one; it was built upon the old site.

THE COMMITTEES.

The Chairmanships of the different Committees were assigned as follows: Preamble and Bill of Rights—Wm. Hutchinson, of Lawrence. Executive Department—John P. Greer, of Shawnee. Legislative Department—Solon O. Thacher, of Lawrence. Judicial Department—Samuel A. Kingman, of Brown Co. Military—James G. Blunt, of Anderson Co. Electors and Elections—P. H. Townsend, of Douglas. Schedule—John T. Burris, of Johnson. Apportionment —H. D. Preston, of Shawnee. Corporations and Banking—Robert Graham, of Atchison. Education and Public Institutions—W. R. Griffith, of Bourbon Co. County and Township Organizations—John Ritchey, of Topeka. Ordinance and Public Debt—James Blood, of Lawrence. Finance and Taxation—Benj. F. Simpson, of Lykins. Amendments and Miscellaneous—S. D. Houston, of Riley Co. Federal Relations—T. S. Wright, of Nemaha Co. Phraseology and Arrangements—John J. Ingalls, of Atchison.

I have studied the composition of these Committees with some interest, reviewing the work of their members in the Convention, and recalling their subsequent careers. And it appears to me that in making them up, President Winchell exhibited phenomenally quick and accurate judgment of men. He was, indeed, one of the best presiding officers I have ever known. His imperturbable coolness, never for an instant ruffled by the most sudden and passionate outbreaks of excitement in the Convention; his mastery of all the niceties of parliamentary law; his uniform courtesy and tact; his promptness and clearness in stating his decisions; and above all, the mingled grace and kindness and firmness with which he announced to an indignant member an adverse decision, were really wonderful. But what shall be said of that still more wonderful prescience with which he made up the Committees? What induced this calm, grey-eyed, observing little man, whose brass-buttoned blue coat was first seen by two-thirds of the Convention on the morning of the 5th of July—what impelled him, within twenty-four hours, to select an obscure, dull-looking, shock-headed country doctor as Chairman of the Military Committee, and thus name in connection with military affairs, for the first time, the only Kansas soldier who reached a full Major Generalship? How did he happen to pass by half a dozen more widely known lawyers, and appoint as Chairman of the Judiciary Committee, a man who, during more than fifteen years thereafter, occupied a place on the Supreme Bench of the State, for the greater portion of this time as the Chief Justice? How came he to recognize so quickly, in the Engrossing Clerk of the Territorial Legislature, the ripest scholar and the fittest man in the body for the Chairmanship of the Committee to which every article of the Constitution was referred for final revision and amendment? In the youngest and most boyish-looking member he found the man who was to form, for this State, a code of Finance and Taxation whose clear directions and wholesome restrictions have guarded Kansas against the wasteful extravagance of Legislatures and the curse of a burdensome public debt, during all the tempting and perilous affairs of its first quarter of a century. And he named, as head of the Committee on Education, the first State Superintendent of Public Instruction. All of his appointments were made with rare judgment, but those mentioned appear notably discerning.

PROGRESS OF WORK.

On the sixth day a resolution favoring biennial sessions of the Legislature—adopted sixteen years afterward—was submitted and referred. The first of a long series of resolutions or proposed sections of the Constitution, prohibiting the settlement of negroes or mulattoes within the limits of the State, was also introduced. This question, with others of a kindred nature, such as propositions to prohibit colored children attending the schools, or to exclude them from the University, or to forbid the appropriation of any funds for their education, and last, and meanest of all, to deny to negroes the shelter of county poor houses when poor and helpless, was voted upon again and again, first in one form and then in another, and to the enduring honor of the majority, always defeated. It seems singular, in this day and generation, that such theories found persistent and earnest advocates. But it should be remembered that all this happened before the war, when slavery was still an "institution" in nearly half the States of the Union. The pro-Slavery party was, of course, solidly in favor of excluding free negroes from the State, and less than four years prior to the meeting of the Convention, the Free State party, in voting on the Topeka Constitution, had given a decided majority in favor of such exclusion. It therefore required genuine courage and principle to go upon record against each and every proposition of this character. For very few members who so voted felt absolutely certain of the endorsement of their constituents.

The first Article of the Constitution reported, that on Corporations and Banks, was submitted on the sixth day and considered. It was stated, by the President, that many other Committees had their reports in the hands of the printer, and during the next few days they began to come in very rapidly. The Convention, to expedite work, adopted a resolution requiring all Committees to report on or before Saturday, the eleventh day of the session.

THE BOUNDARIES OF THE STATE.

On the seventh day the annexation of that portion of Nebraska lying south of the Platte river, was formally considered. The then organized Nebraska counties included in that section of our sister State had elected delegates to the Convention, who were present earnestly advocating annexation. This proposition was discussed during several days, and the debates took a wide range. The Nebraska delegates were admitted to seats as honorary members, with the privilege of speaking on this subject. The final determination, however, was to preserve the original Northern line. Two influences induced this decision, one political, the other local and material. Many Republicans feared that the South Platte Country was, or would be likely to become, Democratic. Lawrence and Topeka both aspired to be the State Capital, and their influence was against annexation, because they feared it would throw the center of population far north of the Kaw.

The Preamble and Bill of Rights was reported on the tenth day, and opened the whole question of the State's boundaries. The Committee proposed the twenty-third meridian as the western line, and the fortieth parallel as the line on the north. This would have excluded about ninety miles of territory within the present limits of the State. The Committee's recommendation was, however, adopted, and stood as the determination of the Convention until the day before the final adjournment, when Col. May, of Atchison, secured a reconsideration, and on his motion the twenty-fifth parallel was substituted for the twenty-third. The northern boundary question was finally settled on the fifteenth day, when, by a vote of 19 ayes to 29 nays, the Convention refused to memorialize Congress to include the South Platte country within the limits of Kansas.

FEATURES OF THE CONSTITUTION.

On the seventh day the Legislative and Judicial Committees reported. The Legislative article was considered next day. The Committee proposed that bills might originate in either House, but Mr. Winchell submitted a novel amendment, which required all laws to originate in the House of Representatives. This was adopted, notwithstanding the vigorous opposition of Mr. Thacher, the Chairman of the Committee, by a vote of 37 to 13. It survived the admission of the State only three years, being amended in 1864.

On the eighth day the Militia article was adopted; on the ninth day the Judicial article was perfected, and the article on Education and Public Institutions reported and discussed; and on the tenth day the Committees on County and Township Organizations, and Schedule, reported. The deathless pertinacity of a "claim" is illustrated by a petition presented that day, from one Samuel A. Lowe, a clerk of the so-called "Bogus Legislature," who wanted pay for certain work he alleged he had performed. Only a year ago Mr. Lowe presented the same claim to Congress, and it was, I believe allowed by the House. But the Kansas Senators made such determined war on it that Mr Lowe can still sing, "a claim to keep I have."

I have mentioned the fact that Mr Winchell was the author of the section providing that all bills should originate in the House. It should be stated that Mr. Ingalls was the author of the provision that "in actions for libel, the truth may be given in evidence to the jury, and if it shall appear that the alleged libelous matter was published for justifiable ends, the accused shall be acquitted." Another original provision of the Constitution is the Homestead section. This was first proposed by Mr. Foster, of Leavenworth county, on the sixth day of the session, and reported by the Committee on Miscellaneous and Amendments, on the thirteenth day. No other feature of the Constitution, perhaps, elicited more animated and earnest debate. It was discussed for several days; amended, referred, and again submitted. As originally reported, it provided for the exemption of "a homestead of 160 acres of land, or a house and lot not exceeding $2,000 in value, or real, personal and mixed property not exceeding $2,000, to any family." This was adopted by a vote of 28 ayes to 16 nays. Two days later the vote was reconsidered, and President Winchell proposed the wording finally adopted: "A homestead of 160 acres of farming land, or of one acre within the limits of an incorporated town or city, occupied as a residence by the family of the owner, together with all the improvements on the same, shall be exempted from forced sale under any process of law, and shall not be alienated without the joint consent of husband and wife, where the relation exists." Thus perfected, it was adopted by a vote of 33 to 7.

I thought at the time, however, and a review of the proceedings and debates has confirmed my impression that favorable action on this provision was due to the earnest and eloquent advocacy of Judge Kingman, who was its most zealous, logical and courageous supporter. The homestead clause of the Kansas Constitution has been severely criticised, but I believe the people of the State generally regard it as a most beneficent provision of their organic law. For nearly a quarter of a century it has been maintained, and it still stands, as Judge Kingman said it would, guarding "the home, the hearthstone, the fireside around which a man may gather his family with the certainty of assurance that neither the hand of the law, nor any, nor all of the uncertainties of life, can eject them from the possession of it."

The Finance and Taxation and the Executive articles were adopted on the fourteenth day, and the Miscellaneous article considered. This originally provided for the election of a Public Printer, but that section was stricken out, after a vigorous protest by Messrs. Ross and Ingalls. Nine years later their idea was endorsed, by the adoption of an amendment creating the office of State Printer.

On the seventeenth day the temporary Capital was located at Topeka, the second ballot resulting: for Topeka, 29; for Lawrence, 14; for Atchison, 6.

THE FIRST "PROHIBITION AMENDMENT."

On the same day a proposition was made, by Mr. Preston, of Shawnee Co., to amend the Miscellaneous article by adding the following section:

"Sec. —. The Legislature shall have power to regulate or prohibit the sale of alcoholic liquors, except for mechanical and medicinal purposes."

A motion made to lay this amendment on the table, was defeated, by a vote of 18 ayes to 31 nays. But the anxiety of the members to exclude from the Constitution any provision that might render its adoption doubtful, or prevent the admission of the State, finally prevailed, and after a full interchange of views, Mr. Preston withdrew his amendment. There is, it is said, nothing new under the sun. Those who imagine that the prohibition amendment adopted in 1880 was a new departure in Constitution making, have never examined the records of the Wyandotte Convention.

THE LAST OF SLAVERY IN KANSAS.

On the nineteenth day occurred the last struggle over the Slavery question in Kansas. Sec. 6 of the Bill of Rights, prohibiting Slavery or involuntary servitude, came up for adoption, and it was moved to add a proviso suspending the operation of this section for the period of twelve months after the admission of the State. This proviso received eleven votes, and twenty-eight were recorded against it. A most exciting discussion occurred, on the same day, over the apportionment article, which the Democrats denounced as a "gerrymander."

THE LAST DAYS.

The work of the Convention was practically completed on the twenty-first day. The various articles had each been considered and adopted, first in Committee of the whole, then in Convention, then referred to the Committee on Phraseology and Arrangement, and, after report of that Committee, again considered by sections and adopted. But so anxious were the members that every word used should be the right word, expressing the idea intended most clearly and directly, that when the reading of the completed Constitution was finished, on the morning of the 21st day, it was decided to refer it to a special committee, consisting of Messrs. Ingalls, Winchell, Ross and Slough, for further revision and verification. This Committee reported the same afternoon, and again the Constitution was read by sections, for final revision, with the same painstaking carefulness and attention to the minutest details. All that afternoon, and all the next day, with brief interruptions for action on other closing work, this revision went on, and it was five o'clock in the afternoon of the 29th before the last section was perfected. Then occurred one of the most dramatic scenes of the Convention. Mr. Hutchinson submitted a resolution declaring that "we do now adopt and proceed to sign the Constitution."

A SPIRITED DEBATE.

At once Mr. Slough addressed the Chair, and after warmly eulogizing the general features of the Constitution, pronouncing it "a model instrument," he formally announced that political objections impelled himself and his Democratic associates to decline attaching their signatures to it. These objections he stated at length. They were, briefly: the curtailment of the boundaries of the State; the large Legislative body provided for; the exclusion of Indians made citizens of the United States, from the privilege of voting; the registry of voters at the election on the Constitution; the refusal to exclude free negroes from the State; and the apportionment.

This action of the Democratic members had been foreshadowed for several days, but it was, nevertheless, something of a surprise. The Republicans understood that several of the Democrats had earnestly opposed such a course, and hoped that some of them would be governed by their own convictions, rather than by the mandate of their caucus. For a few moments after Mr. Slough concluded, the Convention sat, hushed and expectant. But no other Democratic member rose. It was evident that the caucus ruled. Then Judge Thacher, the President *pro tem.*, addressed the Chair, and in a speech of remarkable vigor and eloquence, accepted the gauge of battle thrown down. "Upon this Constitution," he declared, "we will meet our opponents in the popular arena. It is a better, a nobler issue than even the old Free State issue. They have thrown down the gauntlet; we joyfully take it up." He then proceeded to defend, with great earnestness and power, the features of the Constitution objected to by Mr. Slough. "The members of the Convention," he asserted, "have perfected a work that will be enduring." The Constitution, he affirmed, would "commend itself to the true and good everywhere, because through every line and syllable there glows the generous sunshine of liberty." It was and should be, he declared:

"Like some tall cliff, that lifts its awful form,

Swells from the vale, and midway leaves the storm;

Though round its breast the rolling clouds shall spread,

Eternal sunshine settles on its head."

Read in the light of subsequent history, these declarations appear almost prophetic.

19

SIGNING THE CONSTITUTION.

The twilight shadows were gathering about Wyandotte when this debate closed, and the Convention proceeded to vote on Mr. Hutchinson's resolution, which was adopted by 34 ayes to 13 nays—one Republican and four Democrats being absent. The roll was then called, and the Constitution was signed by all the Republican members except one, Mr. Wright, of Nemaha, who was absent, sick. The work of the Convention was completed, and after voting thanks to its officers, it adjourned without date.

TWO MISTAKES.

Each party, I think, was guilty of one blunder it afterwards seriously regretted —the Republicans in refusing to include the South Platte country within the boundaries of Kansas; the Democrats in refusing to sign the Constitution they had labored diligently to perfect. I speak of what I consider the great mistake of the Republicans with all the more frankness because I was, at the time, in hearty sympathy with their action; but I feel confident that no Republican member is living to-day who does not deplore that decision. And I am equally confident that within a brief time after the Convention adjourned, there were few Democratic members who did not seriously regret their refusal to sign the Constitution.

"ADDED TO THE STARS."

On the 4th of October, 1859, the Constitution was submitted to the people for ratification or rejection, and, for the first time in the history of Kansas, all parties cast a full, free and unintimidated vote. The Republicans favored, and the Democrats generally opposed its adoption. Nearly 16,000 ballots were polled, of which 10,421 were for, and 5,530 against the Constitution. The Homestead clause, submitted as an independent proposition, was ratified by a vote of 8,788 for, to 4,772 against it. Every county in the territory except two, Johnson and Morris, gave a majority for the Constitution.

Two months later, December 6th, State and County officers and members of the Legislature were elected, and the people of Kansas, having exhausted their authority in State building, patiently awaited the action of Congress. On the 11th of April, 1860, the House of Representatives voted, 134 to 73, to admit Kansas as a State, under the Wyandotte Constitution. Twice, during the next eight months, the Senate defeated motions to consider the Kansas bill, but on the 21st of January, 1861, several Southern Senators having seceded, Mr. Seward "took a pinch of snuff" and called it up again. It passed by a vote of 36 to 16, and on the 29th of the same month President Buchanan approved it. Thus young Kansas, through many difficulties and turmoils, was "added to the Stars."

AN ENDURING CONSTITUTION.

During nearly twenty-two of the most eventful and exciting years of American history, the Constitution thus framed and ratified has defined the powers and regulated the duties of the government of Kansas. Three Legislatures have voted down propositions to call a new Constitutional Convention. Twelve or fifteen amendments have been submitted, but only eight have been approved by the people. Finally, in 1880, the Legislature voted to submit a proposal for a new Convention, and at the regular election held in November of that year, this ballot was taken. The result was an endorsement of the old Wyandotte Constitution by a majority far more emphatic and overwhelming than that by which it was originally adopted, the vote standing 22,870 for, and 146,279 against the proposed Convention, or nearly seven to one.

It is doubtful whether the organic law of any other State in the Union has more successfully survived the mutations of time and inconstant public sentiment, and the no less fluctuating necessities of a swiftly developing Commonwealth. Of its seventeen articles, only four, and of its one hundred and seventy-eight sections, only eight, have ever been amended. And of the eight amendments adopted, only five have revoked or modified the principles or policy originally formulated, the others being changes demanded by the growth of the State, or by the events of the civil war. The first amendment, ratified in 1861, provides that no banking institution shall issue circulating notes of a less denomination than $1—the original limitation being $5. In 1864 the provision requiring all bills to originate in the House of Representatives, was repealed; and a section intended to prevent U. S. soldiers from voting, but which was so worded that it deprived our volunteers of that right, was also repealed. In 1867 an amendment was adopted disfranchising all persons who aided the "Lost Cause," or who were dishonorably discharged from the army of the United States, or who had defrauded the United States or any State during the war. In 1868 the State Printer amendment was ratified. In 1873 the number of Senators and Representatives, originally limited to 33 and 100, respectively, was increased to 40 and 125. In 1875 three propositions, each having in view biennial instead of annual sessions of the Legislature, were adopted. And in 1880 the Prohibition amendment was ratified. These are all the changes that have been made in our organic law during nearly a quarter of a century.

PARTING AT WYANDOTTE.

It would violate the proprieties of such an occasion to comment on the personal feuds or partisan broils which once or twice marred the general harmony and orderly progress of the proceedings. These were very few, indeed, and none of them, I think, outlasted the Convention. The members parted, when the final adjournment came, with mutual respect and good will, and the friendships formed during the session have been unusually warm and enduring.

SUBSEQUENT HISTORY.

It seems fitting that, in concluding this sketch of the Convention and its labors, I should briefly narrate the subsequent history of its members. It was a small company, that which parted here twenty-three years ago to-day, and it was made up, as I have said, largely of young and vigorous men. But when this reunion was first suggested, and I came to look over the familiar names I had so often called during the long, hot days of that far away July, it was painful to note the havoc death had made. It impressed me something as did a roll-call I once witnessed, in the red glare of bivouac fires after one of the great battles of the war, when surviving comrades answered "killed," or "wounded," to one-half the names of a regiment. Ten of the fifty-two members composing the Convention I have not heard of for many years. Of the remaining forty-two, twenty rest quietly in

—"The reconciling grave,

Where all alike lie down in peace together."

The largest delegation was that from Leavenworth county, and only one of the ten gentlemen comprising it, R. C. Foster, certainly survives. Rare Sam Stinson, whose genial wit and brilliant accomplishments won all hearts, was elected Attorney General in 1861, by a unanimous vote, and died in his old Maine home, in February, 1866. William C. McDowell was chosen Judge of the First Judicial District at the first election under the Constitution; served four years; and was killed by a fall from an omnibus in St. Louis, July 16, 1866. John P. Slough removed to Colorado, was Colonel of a regiment raised in that State, and later a Brigadier General; was appointed, after the war, Chief Justice of New Mexico, and was killed at Santa Fe. Samuel Hipple removed to Atchison county; served as a Quartermaster during the war; was elected State Senator in 1867; and died in January, 1876. William Perry removed to Colorado, where he died. P. S. Parks returned to Indiana, and engaged in journalism and the law until his death, three years ago. Fred. Brown died in St. Joseph, Mo., and John Wright at his home in Leavenworth county. Robert Graham, of Atchison county, the oldest member, died in 1868. Three of the five members from Doniphan county, Robert J. Porter, Benjamin Wrigley and John Stairwalt, are dead. The members from Linn, James M. Arthur and Josiah Lamb, are both dead, as are also N. C. Blood, of Douglas, and T. S. Wright, of Nemaha. W. R. Griffith, of Bourbon, was elected the first State Superintendent of Public Instruction, and died, February 12th, 1862, before the completion of his term. James G. Blunt, of Anderson, who became a Major General during the war, and won renown as a brave and skillful soldier, died, in Washington, a year or more ago. James Hanway, of Franklin, after a long life of usefulness, died at his old home, only a brief while ago. President James M. Winchell returned to New York shortly after the outbreak of the rebellion, and resumed his connection with the *Times*, first as war correspondent and afterwards as an editorial writer. Until his death, a few years since, he was employed upon that great journal.

SURVIVING MEMBERS.

Of the surviving members, many have attained the highest distinctions of the State, and all, I believe are useful and honored citizens. At the first election under the Constitution, Samuel A. Kingman was chosen as Associate Justice of the Supreme Court; in 1866 he was elected Chief Justice, and re-elected in 1872. Benj. F. Simpson was elected the first Attorney General of the State, but resigned the position to enter the army, in which he served throughout the war. He has since been Speaker of the House of Representatives, several times a State Senator, and is now serving his second term as U. S. Marshal. Solon O. Thacher was chosen District Judge at the first election under the Constitution, has since occupied many positions of honor and responsibility, and is a member of the present State Senate. J. C. Burnett, S. D. Houston and S. E. Hoffman were members of the first State Senate, and Geo. H. Lillie was a member of the first House of Representatives. E. G. Ross was appointed United States Senator in 1866, and elected in 1867, serving until 1871. John J. Ingalls was chosen as State Senator in 1861; was elected United States Senator in 1873, and re-elected in 1879, and is still occupying that distinguished place. John T. Burris was Lieut. Col. of the 10th Kansas, and subsequently District Judge. Wm. P. Dutton, James Blood, L. R. Palmer, John P. Greer and John Ritchey have filled many positions of local trust and prominence, with credit and usefulness. R. C. Foster and John W. Forman are residing in Texas; William Hutchinson lives in Washington; and C. B. McClellan, E. Moore and E. M. Hubbard are still prominent and honored citizens of the counties they represented. My old friend, Col. Caleb May, sole surviving member of the three Free State Constitutional Conventions, lives in Montgomery Co. If Dean Swift was right in saying that "whoever could make two ears of corn, or two blades of grass, to grow on a spot of ground where one grew before, would deserve better of mankind, and do more essential service to his country, than the whole race of politicians," what honor is due this sturdy Kansas farmer, who, during a residence of twenty-eight years in the State, has never—not even in the disastrous seasons of 1860 and 1874— failed to raise a good crop. Even the heroic service he rendered the cause of Freedom during the darkest days of the struggle in Kansas, was less valuable to the State than this practical and triumphant vindication of its soil and climate.

"LOST TO SIGHT."

Stalwart, quiet Wm. McCullough I have not heard of for many years. John A. Middleton, of Marshall Co., was a soldier in the 7th Kansas, removed to Montana in 1864, and I have learned nothing of him since. H. D. Preston, of Shawnee; R. L. Williams, P. H. Townsend and Ed. Stokes, of Douglas; Allen Crocker, of Woodson; A. D. McCune, of Leavenworth; J. H. Signor, of Allen, and J. T. Barton, of Johnson, have all disappeared and left no sign. I know not whether they are living or dead.

THE OFFICERS.

Of the officers of the Convention, queer old George Warren, Sergeant-at-arms of nearly all the early Kansas Legislatures and Conventions, died many years ago. Ed. S. Nash, the Journal Clerk, was Adjutant of the 1st Kansas, and died, some years since, in Chicago. Robt. St. Clair Graham, one of the Enrolling Clerks, was elected Judge of the Second Judicial District in 1866, and died in 1880. Richard J. Hinton, also an Enrolling Clerk, is the editor of the Washington (D. C.) *Gazette*, and a widely known journalist. Werter R. Davis, the Chaplain, was a member of the first State Legislature; was Chaplain of the 12th and Colonel of the 16th Kansas regiments during the war; and is one of the most prominent clergymen of his denomination in the State. S. D. McDonald, printer to the Convention, is still engaged in journalism. J. M. Funk, the door-keeper, and J. L. Blanchard, the Assistant Secretary, I have not heard from or of for many years.

CONCLUSION.

I wish I could sketch more in detail the work and history of the members of the Convention. But this paper is, I know, already too long. I have tried to tell how our Constitution was made. I could not narrate, within reasonable limits,

> "What workman wrought its ribs of steel,
>
> Who made each mast, and sail, and rope,
>
> What anvils rang, what hammers beat,
>
> In what a forge and what a heat
>
> Were shaped the anchors of its hope."

It is enough to say that the work has proved strong and enduring. Through the groping inexperience of our State's childhood and the still more perilous ambitions of its youth, through the storm of civil war and the calm of prosperous peace, the Wyandotte Convention has justified the confident hopes of its early friends. The most marvelous changes have been wrought in this country since it was framed. The huge brick building in which the Convention held its sessions, long ago crumbled and fell. The distracted, dependent and turbulent Territory has grown to be a peaceful, powerful and prosperous State. Its hundred thousand people have multiplied to a million. Upon its vast and solitary prairies, where then bloomed a wild and unprofitable vegetation, "wherewith the mower filleth not his hand, nor he that bindeth sheaves his bosom," miles of green meadows now glisten with morning dew, and thousands of golden wheat fields shimmer in the noonday sun, and millions of acres of tasseling corn, rustling in the sweet twilight air, tell of harvests so bountiful that they would feed a continent. Every quiet valley and prairie swell is dotted with pleasant homes, where happy children laugh and play and men and women go their busy ways in prosperous content. Eager learners throng eight thousand school houses. Church bells ring in nearly every county from the Missouri to the Colorado line. More than four thousand miles of railway bind town and country, factory and farm and store, into one community. And over all the institutions and activities of this great, intelligent and orderly Commonwealth, broods the genius and spirit of the Wyandotte Convention. Under its ample authority and direction, just and generous laws have maintained the rights of citizenship, given protection to labor and property, stimulated enterprise, multiplied industries, opened to every child and youth the door of school and college, encouraged morality, fostered temperance, protected the weak, restrained the strong, and sternly punished outbreaking crime. And still the sunshine of popular confidence and favor falls upon the Constitution. It has outlived half of its framers, and when, a quarter of a century hence, the last surviving member of the Convention awaits the inevitable hour, the Wyandotte Constitution may yet be the chart and compass ordering and guiding the destinies of a State whose imperial manhood is foreshadowed by its stalwart and stately youth.